WHAT I TEXTED *HER* LAST TIME?

BY NAVJOT SINGH

WHAT I TEXTED HER LAST TIME?

This is a nonfiction book, presenting real events, people, and facts rather than a fictional story

For permissions contact: {navjotchahal916@gmail.com}

ISBN: 978-93-343-5121-7 (paperback)

My Last texts to *Her*

Preface

Thank You for giving this book your valuable time and I hope you are going to enjoy this walkthrough to the finale where I finally made my confession.

"It was 2017 when I unintentionally planted the seeds of love, and as it grew, it filled my life with fragrance that always reminds me of her"

and just like that the whole pathway is filled with such beautiful flowering plants, I tried my best to make you smell the same Aroma as you take steps into it.

Your attention please

In this book, I talked about confessions and their role in our lives but it's not discussed in order to influence anybody. It was my experience that I had shared and if you want to get something out of it is completely your choice because my only purpose is providing you with one good story to read.

There's one more thing that I would like to make clear, this book gossips about the phases that I lived before doing the confession and how I done it, but it will not explore the further territory What happened next? What's her reply to it? etc. these questions can be answered in another book but not this time...

Now you are free to flip the page and ahead you will look at

'A beautiful memory'

The memory which shines among other pieces of memory shelf

The FIRST Phase

Fueled up, making decision and respecting time

(Step 1)

HAVE TO CONFESS SOMEDAY

Not every Romeo finds voice for his heart's yearning. The act of confession, romanticized in tales, is but one facet of emotional expression. Many burdened by internal reservations or the weight of external realities. It's a fallacy to assume every heart, like Romeo's readily vocalizes his desires.

But when you have the Time, the Moment that feels like some sacred powers has created for you and that Special Person is also near you then dude just say it, PLEASEEEEE

Don't worry about what will happen next. Certainly, here I would like to give you some advice i.e. Do not cross the limits or create such scene that makes the person uncomfortable. Because hearing your feelings was unexpected, as they had never considered it from you.

On the other hand, if you take risk or you share your emotions, then maybe he/she feel uneasy at that time, nevertheless you don't need to be scared. Even though, you know this precious time will never come again or your internal voice says that this is the moment you were waiting for, then without wasting any time just confess *gracefully*.

I know some people who do not like to articulate, What I feel for you, they always regret in future. Honestly speaking, Initially I always trying to be a hard man. According to my mindset a man never share his thoughts, feelings and secrets. He will be died without disclose his sentiments. And no one will be made aware. While I was wrong. All my efforts to become hard went to waste. Here's the evidence before I telling it to you, I had already express my emotions with two of my friends, actually three, if I count her whom I really feels for. For the reason that, I had understood that confession promote self-awareness and accountability, leading to personal growth and positive behaviour changes. It shows that a person is willing to be vulnerable, and that he values the relationship.

...

It's been Three and half years without seeing her. Now we do not have those long talks like we used to have when we were classmates, just a few messages exchanged about our social lives. But it was even worse one year ago when months passed without even opening each other's chat boxes.
We used to just wish each other on our birthdays that's it. But last year when I did not receive her wish, I felt like my birthday did not end properly or it's like I skipped celebrating my birthday this year. Thinking of this incidence for many days and figuring out what I did wrong to her. It forced me to text her...

I want to know –

Why you do not want to wish me –

Or you just forget it –

And She replied that She forgot about it because she was extremely Sick and She's apologized for that and wished me.

After checking on her health, I texted "*Meet Me*" with an hourglass emoji.

Why an Hourglass ⌛ ?

This was a Reminder, reminding her that I was waiting. Waiting for her to come someday and meet me. I didn't know the actual date, but as far as I remember, it was way back in time when I said her, "I want to see you, just tell me whenever you have free time in your schedule" and still up to this day, I am waiting for her to find some time for Me. So that's the reason I use hourglass for.

And after this talk, we did not contact each other for more than half of the year. Until I was really getting Mad of holding my emotions that I had buried under five years ago. I recall the night of *17 September* that I spent thinking about her, written some messages but never sent. Just struggling in my own what should I do?

...

When a Man starts questioning what he truly feels and what he really expects from his life. He mentally maps out multiple approaches to reach his objectives, thinking through 'this option versus that option' and their respective consequences. It can be anything: his respect, his love, the person he speaks to infrequently, or a significant moment, because one wrong turn will take you far from your destination and the path you came from. While in reality, none of those things happen because he steps back: he doesn't want to lose.

(Step 2)

AND WHAT I DONE

Next Day, I decided to revive our bond and without thinking much I dropped "*Hey*", she texted me back and after checking on each other, I came to know, she returned from hospital and She had some tests there, luckily her reports were okay.

Her texts made me think If this is the correct time to say anything because I didn't want her to take any stress and eventually, I texted her ...

I am very confused what should I say to You –

her – Why 😂😂

I really want to talk to you but now I just got blank –

her – 😂😂

I am Serious –

Tell me honestly, do you feel uncomfortable while talking to me? –

I don't know if I should ask this or not –

her – You do not look right to me 😂😂

(Her Name) 😂😂 –

her – I am saying Mentally, not in other way

Your emojis look so good –

I am not looking like weirdo after typing like this, right? –

And after a long time, I felt we had a healthy conversation. Still, I wanted to give her a hint, why I actually texted her or what I really wanted to say. I carried on the conversation and keep acting like a dumb or maybe just I was feeling like this, and finally I managed to say something...

"I want to know if our bond will be again like the one, we had when we were in 10th standard, I know there must be many reasons why everything got changed and you met many new persons, no doubt I will not receive as much importance as they get now. I don't know what I am speaking, If I had ever done something please tell me, I just want there should be no miss understandings and if you have you own personal reasons then also its okay. I know the same connection cannot be built again but still if you allow, we will at least revisit those moments? Whatever I am texting here it's just about You and Me, not any third person. Just don't block me"

On which she replied, she appreciates that I asked her, but currently She's focused on making her career, and I already know what happened with them. After this I wished her best for her future and said if she ever got time then tell me, at least we can talk over a phone call.

25th September

Continuity leads to Success, that's what I was thinking when I texted her.

I just wanted her to feel my presence and give me some importance. She didn't even know how much I was waiting for her call from past 6 days and this one thought keeps making me unhappy that she didn't even call me once, I told her, I want her back in my life but still she's ignoring me.

...

Why I am not the main character in her life even when I have been thinking about her from dawn till dusk. Inwardly it made me feel like I was so caring but when you face reality and you stop living in a house of clouds, you realize I am selfish. Just because I am texting her my emotions which I feel very cute, does not mean she felt the same way and here all the game changes because when two people thinking in other directions, one of them will ends with getting nothing.

So, I decided to take a step back and let the things play on their own for now, and for the call I said

I will wait for that moment –

Just do not make me wait too much –

(Step 3)

GOT THE B'DAY ADVANTAGE

her – Wishing you a very happy birthday, may Waheguru ji bless you with abundance of success and happiness in your life, stay blessed 😊 🎊

Thank you –

I was thinking maybe today I will receive your call –

Are you thinking the same?

*Laughing

Dude I literally took advantage of that moment. Obviously, it's my birthday I knew she won't spoil it and as I thought she will say something else rather than I will call you someday and everything happened as I planned; she got ready to for it. But I had to wait for this night to pass out and the next day to rise with a gift of her voice.

Well, I took it without any argument and after all I wanted to hear her. Over these many months I went through variety of moods, I went from sad and broken, thinking about her at nights when I was all alone and blessing her wherever She is just stay happy, to angry and selfish, blaming the God for not taking my side to and sometimes being a manifester and draws our story in my head if at that time I said this then maybe today will be like this.

I guess everybody went from this phase at some point in their lives. But now the most important question is when she will be on the call, what would I speak?

I was so baffled, even now when I am writing this portion. I can't decide what's the best thing I can say which will bring us a little closer, Maybe I should talk about that phase of our school time when we started knowing each other and accepting our feelings or maybe when we had become really good friends and spent most of the time together or maybe when we were used to go outside with our group or should I confess what I really feels for her.

It's a suspense for me too...

(Step 4)

MY PHONE WAS RINGING

The Night had gone and the next Day had come, the day of make or break. Honestly, I was excited but I had a feeling deep down that she might not call me, even though I trusted her, I realized that our bond was not as strong as it used to be.

Well, I did not have to guess all day about her call because I got it pretty early.

I didn't remember the exact time; I even checked my call log but it did not held that long history. But I am sure it was around 2 p.m. When my phone was ringing, I picked it up and the screen was displaying her name. It put on huge smile on my face and I swiped up to answer her call.

At first, we both were silent like we were waiting for the Hello to come from other side. But for me that few seconds were acknowledgment of the moment that finally *She is here* and then the *Hello* came from her side, it makes me burst in laugh. I cannot explain what exactly I was feeling at that time. It was something like I was running in a garden, whose gardener was a divine figure because everywhere I was seeing colourful flowers with an adorable fragrance that made me feel like I had lost control over thinking, just flowing in the seas of floral beauty and the illusion breaks when she asked me *What happen* and I remember she was laughing too.

I had no words to explain her, what's happening to me. I don't know those words. I reminded myself that this time will not come again, so I came out of the sugar river and continued the conversation. After few minutes when formalities had been done it's time to ask something meaningful and I ask her about her life, what she's doing and what she's planning for future. Her words were full of motivation and her vibes were utterly optimistic, that the way she was speaking made it seem as if, having set herself on the right path, she knew that day wasn't for holding back. If she pushes herself, she will run alongside success, and if she goes a little further, success will chase her.

...

I knew that she faced a lot of issues (i.e. family, financial, and personal). Maybe at some point she got broken because what's happening in her life was completely opposite to what she had planned. I may get wrong in understanding her issues but I am definitely not wrong when I am saying that...

She's never down and out, there's no way life can pin her. She may get out of picture for some time but she never stay there for long. She knows how to come back and proves to life; she is still standing.

Sometimes I wonder, from where she's getting all the motivation, the courage and the confidence to carry on the fight, answer is really very simple and if we adopt this in our lives than half of our troubles will just disappear, we can actually see those troubles were just created in our heads and never existed in real. So, what she's actually doing?

She has surrendered herself to the Akal Purakh, which means all her sorrows is no longer belong to her, whatever the Almighty will choose for her is her destination. Her unwavering faith, undeniable respect she carries for her spiritual master give her a bed of relief even when she's surrounded with pain.

One thing I would like to clear about her i.e. it's me who is saying she is fighting, she is facing issues, she's having pain but from her point of view it's not the pain or sorrow or any fight she's having because she knows this is life, she never blames or cry about it. Because she has the power to accept Bhana.

What is Bhana?

In Sikhism, Bhana is a significant concept that can be defined as God's will, His order or whatever He likes or sees fit and how we should accept his bhana? (ਤੇਰਾ ਭਾਣਾ ਮੀਠਾ ਲਾਗੈ) "Tera Bhana Meetha Laage" is written in Gurmukhi as "Your Will Tastes Sweet (as Nectar)". It is a Gurbani shabad that means everything happens according to God's will, and that God's will is always sweet.

...

Her words totally changed the mood and time and that day if I choose to confess her then maybe I will picture myself as selfish in my own eyes because the level of concentration she's having, I didn't want to mess it up.

So, I chose to stay quiet and let the conversation happened on its own and this reached to one of the questions which I really wanted to ask, can't we be those friends which we used to be five years ago? On which she said time changed her a lot and there's no point going back from where we came from and I totally understand this. After this I just went blank, I had nothing left to say and eventually we had to end that call.

All the things that I had planned to say were just went like they never existed.

STEPPING BACK? Phase

Shifts, Disruption and Holding

(Step 5)

THE TIME HAD COME

Of what? I don't want to keep you guys in dark, like you can see the chapter name and expect maybe now the time has come to confess her but it's not about that. It's actually the time to take a step back.

Before knowing it's reason, I guess you guys should know My January went so well, maybe I got everything what I longing for these many months and who knows those moments will ever come again or not. So, I am really happy what I had received and do not expecting anything else now.

I got to interact with her, Three times. I had already told you about the first two but this last interaction gave me a very special what can I call it a gift or moment. I will tell you everything but before that I want you to know what I felt for that moment so you can come to my emotion level

The moment I am talking about with so much passion was just of few seconds, hardly 5 seconds. But for me those five seconds became longer than any number of hours because I was kind of stuck in that moment, I didn't done it intentionally or making up some love sentences for this book, I was just feeling blessed that I had received something I never expected to receive and I was more than happy that I had those five seconds with me and those were enough for me to live my whole life with and I know I will never come out of it.

What happened in those five seconds?

I remember the date was 21st of January and the time was around 1:30 p.m. I was sitting at the back of scooter and My friend was driving, and we were going to shop a party dress for my friend's office party. We were going from the same route on which we always drive on and I was just talking to my friend about something and I looked forward, I saw a beautiful girl in black dress and I looked in her eyes, she's looking at me too. For a second, I just lost myself, like I was not alive, I was not any living entity, this was not the earth and suddenly when she's passing by, I looked at my right She's none other but the one and only *Her*, whom we were conversating about all this time. We both were on bikes so you understand there's not much time I got to see her but still this is enough, I kept looking back, she's going far and far and I watched her until she gets blurred and I had put a lot of strain on my eyes but it's not their fault, she's just gone.

...

26th March

That was the last time I had seen her in quiet a few years and that phone call was the last time when we had talked to each other. After that we again got busy in our own stuff until one day I received a call from a random number.

I was just lying on my bed and my eyes were closed. It's all dark in my room and time was around 12:18 p.m. I was just free at that day and my phone had started ringing, I checked it and the call was from some unknown number. Usually, I do not receive much calls but this was from a random number. It makes me think who would it be and the answer was just there on other side waiting for me to pick up that call.

I answered the call and surprisingly I heard the sweetest hello of all time. Well, it's not tough for you and me also to guess who would it be? Yes, u guessed it right. My all sleepiness went away and I regained all my energy. Actually, she was calling from her company's phone and asked me If I was interested to do a job.

My very first thought was What would be better than working with her in the same company? This is the best opportunity I can ever get to relive my school days and she will be there in front of my eyes, I can talk to her anytime and sometimes we will go out together. Wow, what a life, bro! So, I asked her what kind of job it is? She said your will be hired as an HR, rest I will explain you in evening about company and it's working.

In the evening

To be honest in those days I was really looking for a job because I wanted to buy myself a new phone and I was thinking if I got selected in her company than it would be like killing two birds with one stone.

Few hours later as she said, I received her call. She explained me everything from company's purpose to their work culture and selection process for freshers. Till now everything seems fine until my inner fears hit me. What if I got rejected by her boss then I will look like a fool, or what if I failed at very beginning test, she will think he is so dumb. But there was no point of tangling myself in unnecessary thoughts, I have to give it a try, I will do my best; rest is my fate.

I was just filling myself with motivation and She just said *but I am here for more like 5 or 6 days, after that I will leave this company.* Wait what then there's no point for me to work their if she's leaving right. Okay I know I need money but I really don't like such company's environment because I had worked for a similar kind of company and that was a horrible experience. There's no way I can say No to her but you can understand. So, I just shared my experience to her and She understood it because she's also leaving because of work load and environment.

That was really a good chance to meet her but What can I do now, maybe some other day, at some better place. Still, this was not the climax, I texted her a sorry message and trying to tell her if she has any kind of need, just let me know, and I will be there, we just started talking there.

Everything was going same as always until she texted something that I did not expected to come, I mean at that time otherwise I knew this could be a possibility.

I was just asking her to meet me and taunting her...

Meet me someday please –

her – Don't worry we will meet

– When the time will come

Oh yes –

I know that time will never come in your clock –

her – 😂

Don't laugh –

her – 🙄

if someone else asked you this much, you would probably met him numerous times –

her – whom 😂 😂

Who knows... only you know that and why will you tell me –

her – Sadly I can't he is not here 😂 😩

I should stop here. I guess this is enough to understand what's happening. Yeah so, I kind of knew that maybe she likes someone or maybe she's in a relationship and there's nothing wrong obviously we both are living different life. Now that's another thing, I am struggling to forget *Her*, I just wanted to speak out the whole truth and just walked away, I was happy where my life's taking me.

I was actually happy for her, because love is the strongest emotion and if it done correctly, I mean selflessly then it will be your strength and this is not surprising at all, when everybody getting boyfriends and girlfriends then She's also one of us. I did not asked her much about her love or relation because I didn't want to make her uncomfortable or force her to made up any excuse why she can't tell me. Right, why do I create such situation where I know I am not getting any result. I don't play in those games where I know I can't win.

At that time, I decided that whatever I have for her is going to be in between me and my heart, I believe there's very thin line between confessing and running after somebody whom you want to make part of your life or be a part of their life and I am standing on the confessing side. I know you may think there's no point of confession when she love somebody else but I wanted to do justice to my five years ago self. I didn't want her to be my something. I just wanted her to know I fell in love with her at that time and I just want her to remember me always. I just knew I will regret my whole life if I never told her about my emotions. As I told you I just want to confess her and did not expecting anything in return and I believe confessions will give you peace. You, your soul can happily live without carrying any weights of hiding and after all this is the only life we are living as ourselves. So, I guess we should live our life at our best.

Maybe this writing will not justify what I really want to convey but I do not know any better words, I am sorry for that.

(Step 6)

I CAN NOT HOLD IT ANYMORE

Human will always be a human, I convinced myself that from now, I am not going to think anything about confessing her or meeting her and why should I? it was in past and I really do not want to do anything with it now or in future. So, it does not matter if she knows it or not.

I was just moulding my thoughts and it was working for me. I always heard a man should have full control over his thoughts and feelings, and it's actually true. For a peaceful life one should learn it because all the anger, unsatisfaction, jealousy, vengeance and many more internal issues, these all generated from our own feelings. But it only seems easy when you are advising somebody, when it comes to you, maybe you will do more worse than those whom you are advising. I am just talking about myself, so do not get offended.

Everything was going smooth but still my last message to her was ...

I know you are not going to speak anything now... what I want to say for last time, will tell you when we will meet.

I just want to meet her one time so I can tell her everything that I wanted to, this message kept provoking me to speak out every single word I thought, I wrote and I devoted to her. Do not judge me I felt that five years ago, so I really have a lot to say.

Still, I was trying to keep myself busy so I did not get any time to think about it. But I am also a human, I just got tired expecting from future that one day destiny will arrange something for me where I can confess her everything. I am just done, for how long I can stop the water from flowing into its direction, we all know that, at the end of the day, the water will throw me away as it flows freely.

And just like that, my stream of emotions break all the walls I have built and reached where they want to, to *Her.*

(Step 7)

THAT DAY WAS NOT SAME AS ALWAYS

The wait is over, I tried everything.

I tried to find flaws in her. But I failed to find any.

I even left everything on Almighty, like he will plan a date for us. 😂

I pretend to be a man of big heart and acted as let her go and let her be happy.

I tried to explain myself that it was just my past. I was a kid at that time; it does not matter now.

I forced myself into other things so I can't get any time to think about her and eventually one day I will forget everything.

But I failed miserably, I had enough now. I am not going to hide from it or run from it anymore. I will just tell her and became free and afterwards if she like to stay as a friend or want to block me that's her choice, I will never complain about it and this chapter will be closed forever.

The CONFESSION Phase

Calculated, Framed and Poured heart out

"I will not wait for her to meet me; Today I will text her my confessions

and whatever will happen next, I will deal with it."

(Step 8)

AND I TEXTED HER

This might be the last time I was texting her, So I wanted it to be perfect. I wanted the start to be engaging, which will interest her to continue reading what I had written.

And here I would like to give credit to my brother like friend, he kind of giving me pumps to text her. 😂 and me who got hyped and planned with him how I will be going to start the conversation, it was fun actually.

I came up with sending her, her own old pictures and maybe she will get little surprised and it will give her an impression that this stupid man still owns her five-six years old photos and she maybe ask me, were you looking at my pictures? and I will laugh on it which will confirm her Yes, he was.

What a master plan, right. So, I spent like 1-2 hours, searching for her photos in my computer and I copy pasted her all images. But then I thought if I will send her all the pictures then maybe her attention will get divided, she will look more on the photos and less on my text. I am genius 😂.

Hey –

Today I was looking at my old pictures –

And I found some of yours –

Picture 1 –

Picture 2 –

I sent her the selected photos and waiting for her to see them and reply me something.

Waiting, Waiting and Waiting…still waiting

It's been an hour and I got no reply. She didn't even come online and at that time I just thought, maybe I should skip this thought. But I didn't know why I was feeling the courage that I never felt before. **Today is the day, now or never** and I decided to text her…

(Step 9)

WAIT IS NOT ALWAYS SWEET

It could be sweet; I am just partially agree with it. There are some times when patience could be the best thing you can do, but not every time and this is exactly that time when wait will be costly for me. And I can't choose wait always.

Can we meet someday, Yes but I have to wait for the right time.

Could you please call me when you get free, Days went by and what I am doing just wait.

Hey, I texted her and guess what I am doing next, waiting for her to answer me, for how long? can't say it could be any number of days or she will just ignore it.

Could you please made me those sandwiches that you used to bring in school. Yes, thank you and when I am getting those. Wait.

Sandwiches could be tasty but the wait, ha-ha. I tasted the fruit of wait and in reality, it was not sweet for me.

I told you many times that I want to meet you...I even tried to make you understand many times,

if you never wanted to meet me then you should have told me the first time –

All these years I never said anything so that our little talks that we have after many months

do not get stopped because of it –

So, I rejected to wait this time and honestly, I have no hate for her, for all the wait I received, I will never blame her for that. I believe that's my fate and nobody can do anything in this, and maybe this is the reason that I just confessed her and had not waited for right time. I just lost trust on my destiny.

(Step 10)

OUR CHAPTER

I love our chapter, even though it's not very long,

But the moments in it make a place for you forever

After a few days it comes to my mind, again and again

You were in satsung and when I asked you,

You said I couldn't lie here

How beautiful that time was

This is something that is personal between us and I never talked about it openly because you never wanted me to share it with anyone

After meeting you I just wanted to say,

I know you can never be mine

Whatever the reason or situation

And I also know that I can never have you, not in this life

But I really loved you a lot

And I always will

(Step 11)

I'M SORRY TO YOU...

Sorry, if these messages cause any trouble in your life –

What I wanted from her?

Just sit with me for some time, hear me once what I have to say and whatever happened at that night, share with me what she had actually felt and how did she let it go.

You know she would never agree that she had sacrificed her feelings, so that someone else's feelings wouldn't get hurt. She can never build her home on the ashes of a murdered heart, maybe that's why she has forgotten that time or she has forced herself to forget that time.

And what I am doing? I am forcing her to remember all the painful moments of her life that she had drowned in the ocean so that the waves could never bring them back to her shore. But the ocean has a rule, whatever we throw into it will one day throw back to us.

I don't want my peace if it costs me her happy life.

Because I wanted to confess this to you from many years –

I chose the worst time to do so –

And place also –

Maybe in future you get agreed to meet me, but after all of this you will never agree –

I know u like someone too –

I will always pray that you stay happy in your life –

Just remember me as a person with some unwritten pages left behind –

I'm sorry to you and your partner also –

The NOSTALGIC Phase

Initial Days, Best Moments and Stays forever

(Initial Step 0.1/12)

LOVE AT FIRST SIGHT

The most special thing about love is that it always remains as fresh as the first time it happened. The moment it happened for first time, stays with you till your last breath and if your love got blessed by Almighty then your love will be remembered by this world for many years.

And everything starts from the first sight. There's many times when a person want to give up on their relation but the charm of first sight act as platelets, prevent bleeding and heal the wound to again feel the same love that you felt at the *first sight*.

I remember the first time I felt love for you was –

When you were going somewhere on a bike with your father –

You were wearing a blue green color suit –

I remember I was walking to somewhere and I saw a beautiful face, the sun of evening welcoming her like she's the princess of some divine realm. The wind was ruffling her hair exposing her complete face to me and each millisecond I spent beholding her beauty, making me surrender to her and when she got out of my sight then I realized that she's my classmate bro, I know her...

That time I decided, no bro I need to talk to her –

I want to be in your eyes, want your attention –

That this guy also exists in our class –

😂 –

I was feeling so shy but I need to tell her.

If I want to have her company, want to have conversations with her and really do not want to regret later in life then I have to make a move, and my self-counseling worked well...

And I remember you were in best section class –

I came to you in recess and told you –

You were looking so beautiful and she gave me a smile. Our faces were so close, I looked into her eyes and rest cannot be explained in any words. I can just say...

What a lovely time this would be of my life, if all this had happened while you were sitting in front of me –

Maybe you would have been smiling listening to all my nonsense –

Your heart may not hold any negative memories for me. –

I can imagine –

You placed your arms on a table, one of your hands under your chin, and listening to me –

I want to look into your eyes –

They are so lovely –

Thought of having a personal chapter with you makes me feel so good –

Today after so long I am talking so openly –

(Initial Step 0.2/13)

MUSIC IS LANGUAGE OF LOVE

Those times were great –

We used to dedicate songs to each other…maybe you remember –

Or you just don't want to remember –

Yes 😂, we really use to dedicate songs to one another. 2017- 2019 was just very cool years, on WhatsApp we guys use to forward a message containing ten questions related to us and our friend has to answer them and sometimes in those ten questions the one question was send me a song which you think represent my personality or a song which describe our bond.

We answered such questions many times and we always dedicate something fresh and more like what we actually feel for each other and to be honest these songs were the one which sparked the flame of love. It's our way to convey our feelings, we had never said it in words, maybe because of the fear of losing and the music brings us so close that I eventually fell in love, I can't say about her.

If you ask me, do I remember those songs. No, I don't but I remember one song that she dedicated,

Gulabi Pagg by Diljit Dosanjh

And I remember that time the Gulabi (Pink) turban was my favourite. She might had seen my picture somewhere with pink turban on and this song was maybe to express she liked pink turban on me or she wanted me to know that she's noticing me.

Now don't say it could be coincidence or I am just overthinking it 😂.

(Initial Step 0.3/14)

SECRET OF OUR MATCHING OUTFITS

You remember once on your birthday you wore a white colour dress –

and surprisingly I wore a white kurta pajama, it seemed as if we had deliberately matched our outfits like a couple. But I know she did not even have any hints of this, for her it's just a coincidence and honestly, I won't comment on how she felt about it. But I can claim that I wore the white colour intentionally because...

I asked your best friend what are you wearing this evening –

She said it's a white colour dress with flowers painted on it –

So that's why I wore white and I had tied a sand brown colour turban to match the theme of flowers and I remember, I was trying to impress her and expressing my love, I thought this could be a nice way to show my interest but I cannot justify if it had worked or not 😂.

This is one of my favourite moments I have with her. It is special for two reasons; one is obviously that we were wearing the same colour outfits on her birthday, another is it was the first time for me that I got some pictures clicked with her. I mean I don't know I was feeling so shy and nervous, all that time I was thinking I want some pictures with her, but how could I ask her and somehow, I just did it.

It was back in 2019 and I can still look up at those clicks as the best pictures I have, me and her in one frame, what more I can ask for, it was the best thing happened to me at that time and the reason is quite simple because that time we were on a growing stage of friendship, anything we done for each other had put smile on our faces. Other photos may have good back story but these are like the locked timeframes of my life which can be accessed anytime and it will remind me of the freshness of thoughts, the efforts we were putting in and the fragrance of acceptance. Everything was just perfect.

(Initial Step 0.4/15)

THOSE EXHIBITION DAYS WITH HER

I also love that time when we were making the model together –

Every year in our school there was an exhibition held where students get into the groups and create models based on the provided topics and in the school, *she* was a popular craft person, I mean all the teachers knew this so every teacher wanted her to create a model on their subject and topic.

Don't worry guys your hero was also famous for his fluent English speaking and it is one of the most important elements of model exhibition because to win the prize of the best model you should know how to explain your model.

How we get into the same team?

So, we both had a favourite teacher (*Mrs. Mamta Mam)* she used to teach us English and I can proudly say that I was one of her favourite students. So, she wanted me to create a model which show how much the theatres got upgraded, basically I had to make a theatre of the past and the present to compare both of them. She knew that me and *her* were good friends so she put us in a same team along with our other friends and a group of four was formed (technically five).

The best thing about these days was we can work on our models in the school this means we did not have to study and it provided me so much time to spend with her. I still remember standing next to her, looking at her face, handing things over (during which our fingers for sure got touched), talking with her and sharing food. What a lovely time it was.

I want to relive those days...

(Initial Step 0.5/16)

LANGUAGE OF LOVE

I know this conversation became more like reading out the old diaries but what can I do? All I have in the name of *her* is memories. All I can share is What I had *thought* or *planned* at that time, What I *actually did* and what I *received* back, that's it. These memories became my language of love, and that's why even when I was texting her, I am talking in this language only.

(Her Name) You don't have to think about this all –

I don't want your life to get disturbed by this all –

I don't know why but I felt like this is the time to tell you everything –

Who knows if I'll ever get another chance –

I had actually accepted my fate; I just want to Quit visiting her memories again and again. It's not because I am tired of it, to be honest I love thinking about my old days, I spent in school with my friends or with *her* but this time I again want to start walking; me, my body and my soul we all had enough of rest in the laps of sweet memories and to explore the next chapters of life I need to finish reading my old ones. So, that's why I decided to confess everything to her that night.

I don't want any kind of misunderstanding between you and me, by stop visiting her memories does not mean my love for her will be done, it's just I will preserve it somewhere in the cabinet of my good old memories in the room of my body called heart. I will love her till the end but I do not want it to stop exploring me further life because it's not the end however it will be a beautiful end but still...

Honestly, I am happy that when you came into my life, I found you standing by me in all my important moments. –

I know that you have nothing in your heart for me... and I also know that you will never have it –

This maybe sound strange to you guys like how I am so sure that she does not have any feelings for me now, you may be remember from the Ch.5 (*The Time Had Come*) where she hinted me of somebody, we actually had more talk about that person but I do not want to discuss her personal life here that's why I did not write much about that guy, I will just give you a hint that she loves him now that's it. This is the reason I had texted her that now you will never have any space for me that's actually not a bad thing obviously I am happy that she had found somebody ideal for her and, me I am just happy that I had memories with her and confessed her ...

I really just wanted to talk to you (her name) –

I want to tell you everything that's in my heart –

Over these years, there have been many nights when I've opened your inbox, typed messages but never had the courage to send them –

It's almost midnight when I was texting her and I didn't know what I was texting, when I said one thing and when I started another thing. I had no idea; I just remember I was feeling like drunk without touching any alcohol but *her* name, *her* memories, *her* beauty and this *one-sided Love* have more stronger intoxication that I kept texting her without checking if this message was connected to previous one or if this message make any sense or not.

I don't know about others but for me You are the most beautiful creation of the Creator –

I don't care what my outer life will do to me or how it will affect my other relations –

You know there are some feelings –

Which belongs to you only –

Only you can feel them –

And I have those feelings for you –

And I am happy that these feelings will stay with me forever –

Forever –

❤ –

And with this Red Heart I decided to end my conversation.

The LAST Phase

Difficult, Acceptance and Leave

(Step 17)

IT ALL STARTED WITH A HEY

If this message will shows up to you first then maybe you won't even open the chat 😂 –

So, I will simply send you a hey –

Why I am telling you my plans 😂 –

As I came out of her inbox, I see a red heart is visible because it was the last message, I thought if she will sees it then maybe she won't even open my chat box, right? Maybe she hesitates and do not want to face any situation like this, then I thought let's simply put Hey as a last message so she will took it as causal message and she will open my inbox to reply me.

And I was imagining the whole scenario of next morning that when she will open inbox then she will see so many messages and she will be feeling so good like how even after so long He's still showering so much love and she will reply me, "*oh dear I really loves you too, I do not want anything in life just need a true loving husband like you"* ...Blah! Blah! I was just seeing the dreams with open eyes, I guess we humans manifest a lot but in real those imaginations won't even get touched...Poor human

From now on whenever you see a 'Hey' quickly recognize it as a part of master plan...okay?

Hey –

It all started with a Hey –

(Step 18)

BEAUTIFUL BELONGINGS

Hey –

And yes, I want to thanks you –

For everything you had given me –

It's not about materials –

I am talking about the memories –

And yes, your sandwiches how I can forget them –

Sandwiches 🥪

I could write a whole another book about how much I miss the sandwiches she used to bring to school... My mouth is watering as I am writing about them

I love to cook my favourite dishes and till this date I can't figure out what makes those sandwiches so tasty, is there any secret recipe or ingredient, or is it the love that she puts in while making them.

I remember the first time, in *2017* I had tasted them and oh my god, from that day the Sandwiches become my top favourite pick, that's another thing that I had never found any other sandwich close to the sandwich that she made.

There were many times in school when she brought sandwiches only on my special request, and now the time has completely changed. I asked her many times to please make me that sandwiches once but I never got to taste them again. As I am longing to meet her in the same way I want to have those sandwiches once more.

You remember I asked for a sign pen from you every time before our Exams –

However, I could buy it myself but the pen that you brought especially for me and give it to me –

In what words I can explain that joy –

Back to –

Hey –

These are really small things but it holds the great importance, like sandwiches if she will ever make them again maybe it will reminds her how much I used to love her sandwiches or that pen, maybe if she ever sees that pen, it will remind her about how close we were but I hope she doesn't think about how much money I had wasted on him 😂

For me these little things are so important, I still crave for those sandwiches and that pen whenever I use it, it takes me back to *her*, back to the time when we were more than just friends. Anything which is connected to her is special.

(Step 19)

SHE WOKE ME UP

It was past midnight and I thought it's enough now; I had already texted her over 100 messages and who knows if she will even read them or not and what will be her reaction, I should stop now and I turned off my phone and went to sleep.

It was the peak of summer and in those days, people like to sleep under the open sky. I came out of my room and it was already too late, everything was so quiet and my parents were sleeping and I lay down by their side. I was just wondering if I did it right or should I just go and delete all the messages since nothing had gone wrong yet.

I was choosing my side and I felt as if someone was waking me up. My eyes were closed but I could feel someone close to me, although no one had touched me but I could feel the presence and within a few moments I had felt the harsh light but I remember that night the moon was in its Waning Gibbous phase (this is between a full-moon and half-moon) so it was not possible unless somebody is pointing torch on my face.

I opened my eyes and I saw her, she was flying and wearing something sparkly white with her long hair covering the entire sky, it looked like she was the moon in her black hair and when I woke up, she disappeared.

This was not a long sequence it was just a matter of seconds and I'm not making this up it could be due to a hallucination because where I last saw her, in the same spot the moon was, maybe that night's moon was a beautiful one, you can relate it to anything.

I thought it's a sign that I should text her now only and maybe I am not getting another day for this, and I went back in picked up my phone and the first thing I typed was how beautiful she was looking, there's no other star, no moon, there's nothing with whom I can refer to her beauty...

You know –

You have an adorable smile –

And you are so beautiful –

(Step 20)

ONE LAST SONG

The night I was confessing, is one of the most romantic nights of me. Even physically, she's not there but still I can feel her. It's just me, my feelings and my imagination, we three talking to each other and all talks were about *Her*.

When I was telling her all about me then I thought I should also tell her about my early mornings.

Usually I didn't wake up early, I know it's not a good thing but in the morning my bed kind of hugs me so tight that I just couldn't get up. But there are also some mornings when it does not matter if I have my sleep properly or not because in the night, I drug a lot. These are not any common drugs, you cannot buy them, because how could you buy love or moments with that special person. There are many nights I spent thinking about my love.

All those nights which I devoted to her were not went like other devotional nights when I slept and, in the morning, I woke up and everything felt like a dream only, No. When I spent nights remembering her then even my mornings were not different from nights, I was like playing a single song on loop until somebody came and stopped it.

And in those Mornings, I went up on roof, breathing the fresh air, welcoming the sun, watching the clouds moving on and hearing a special song and the same song I sent her...

Maybe this is the last time so I am dedicating a song to you and us –

Choo lo – Aalas ka Pedh by The Local Train –

I am still Standing where I always did, my heart is restless again.

I am still Standing where I always did, waiting for you to come back.

(Step 21)

THE LAST TEXT

I am not expecting any replies from you, don't reply me because the feelings with which I wrote these messages, I know that you do not have those feelings and it's not your fault I understand that you had and have a life of your own, you have a family, you have your goals, you have a beautiful love and of course you have a relation with him...you really do not need to reply a side character of your movie and I will not feel bad about it because I know that

I do not deserve you –

(Step 1)

DO YOU REALLY NEED TO CONFESS?

The Last Text may sounds like an abrupt end, leave it. Yes, I know that I woke up to text her some more messages and I did write something but I had not discussed them in this book. But I will provide you a hint that the things I had said were nothing out of my old texts, it was just confessions that I had made earlier. So, you can consider it completing a circle and now, **I am standing at the same point where I had started**.

I am Happy that I said her what I wanted to from a long back but to be honest it didn't change my life in any shape or form. These all things I had written, does it affect anybody? nobody cares and today, I am thinking why I had texted her and even I didn't remember it, if this is real or an imagination, The time I confessed her were night so it's just went like I had seen a dream. This is only now added to the shelf, placed alongside other memories.

So, *the Confessions*, do you really need to do? Still, I say Yes, it's part of our life.

We all do confessions and it's not a new thing. If you observe them closely then you will find out that confessions also age like us, it also get matures.

In late childhood, children are more apt to confess. They are more positive about confessing. Even if they lied for first time, they will confess it and try not to repeat it. While in Teenage, the concept of confession gets broader. Now these confessions are not just between a child and a parent, it will now can be done to a friend (depends on what type of confession it is). Next is young adult, this stage is very confused one, one is experiencing a lot of new things which has direct impact on life and actions which made the confessions harder but once he will figure them out, he realizes confessions help to move forward with peace and these confessions can be done to anybody. Finally, an Adult, I think adults do very calculated confessions, and it's important for them to do so cause there one word will make or break a relation for whole life.

So, we cannot sperate the confession from a child or a friend or a partner, even a soul also confess to Almighty. It's just one thing we should consider before confessing to a human that is, will he or she actually going to care about your words or you just making your own fool in front of them. Because confessing is not a bad choice, but if you are doing it on cost of your self-respect then I'll advice you to think twice and even if you think that person will listen to you even then don't expect anything in advance like I had not expected any flowers or stones, so just confess it if your heart is really full of emotions and it's outflowing and damaging rest of body then confess it, just do not pre plan anything let the time play its dice.

The most important thing is, it does not decide your life. She may be happy in her own life and I am living my life at best with no regrets, Akal Purakh had given me everything more than a person like me ever deserved. So, things like this just decorates your life now if you like the decoration or not that's another thing.

I am happy that I met a person like her, but it's fine with me if she didn't stay for longer. Everyone has their own destiny and we can just pray for the best for them.

her – Typing…

MY LAST TEXTS TO HER

a note for my future wife

"Hey Dear, I am sorry."

First thing is I am not betraying you, if you ever came across this just relax, I really loves you and loves you only, that whole thing you red was happened with me at some point of time and I made that girl this confession just to empty the space for you because I do not want you to adjust with anybody and look I am all yours and I will never divide myself into two.

ABOUT THIS BOOK

Hey! I never thought I will see you here my dear reader, it's our first meet maybe and look what we had just talked about *My last texts to her*, sounds like gospel material itself walks over to you right. Well, I will not stop you from gossiping about this 😂.

Actually, I had no plan to form a book. This all started with one change that I was noticing, my memory isn't as sharp as it used to be, my old memories started getting blur and for sure one day it's all getting dark, yes, I know there will be set of candles that keep a little part of story lighten but I do not want to forget my stupid texts.

So, I decided to preserve this moment. There were many ways to do that, like I can take the screenshots get it print. But this is not my way to do things, during those times, I was trying to write one another book and I had done writing it's three chapters but then this all happened and that project went into a corner. But it stayed somewhere inside me that I wanted to write a book, and I thought I had enough content to write this time, every message I texted her, had a back story or some context that I can elaborate. But even that time, I just want to keep it to myself.

One can think from where I should start writing and I guess it's worth spending time on because it can make or break your story but I kept it simple, the first chapter was the first thought and rest of the chapters were written in sequence as things moving forward. When I had formed first few chapters, I saw a path which was welcoming me to take my writing to the town of book readers and I thought to give it a try, I mean maybe it will be a fun, short and sweet book that one can digest while traveling. So, this motivational thought helps to finish writing it under a month or two.

As this book based on real event so I didn't have to worry much about story part and for writing I didn't have much knowledge or experience so I kept the writing simple, but main challenge was grammar and literally I am so bad at it, but when I was writing, I tried to focus more that how I can justify my emotions and how my readers can be at my place and understand what's actually going inside me.

But I consider myself lucky, because I have an elder sister whose insights and support were essential in shaping this story. If this book is in your hands, it could only be possible then, my sister become my co-pilot in this creative adventure. I would like to say a heartfelt thank you to my sister for her wonderful help and for so beautifully demonstrating the strength of sisterhood.

www.ingramcontent.com/pod-product-compliance
Lightning Source LLC
Chambersburg PA
CBHW062147160726
48282CB00027B/950
9789334351217